Acting Edition

D1232737

The Swearing Jar

by Kate Hewlett

║ SAMUEL FRENCH ║

FOR PRODUCTION INQUIRIES

UNITED STATES AND CANADA
info@concordtheatricals.com
1-866-979-0447

UNITED KINGDOM AND EUROPE
licensing@concordtheatricals.co.uk
020-7054-7298

Each title is subject to availability from Concord Theatricals Corp., depending upon country of performance. Please be aware that *THE SWEARING JAR* may not be licensed by Concord Theatricals Corp. in your territory. Professional and amateur producers should contact the nearest Concord Theatricals Corp. office or licensing partner to verify availability.

No one shall make any changes in this title(s) for the purpose of production. No part of this book may be reproduced, stored in a retrieval system, scanned, uploaded, or transmitted in any form, by any means, now known or yet to be invented, including mechanical, electronic, digital, photocopying, recording, videotaping, or otherwise, without the prior written permission of the publisher. No one shall share this title(s), or any part of this title(s), through any social media or file hosting websites.

For all inquiries regarding motion picture, television, online/digital and other media rights, please contact Concord Theatricals Corp.

MUSIC AND THIRD-PARTY MATERIALS USE NOTE

Licensees are solely responsible for obtaining formal written permission from copyright owners to use copyrighted music and/or other copyrighted third-party materials (e.g., artworks, logos) in the performance of this play and are strongly cautioned to do so. If no such permission is obtained by the licensee, then the licensee must use only original music and materials that the licensee owns and controls. Licensees are solely responsible and liable for clearances of all third-party copyrighted materials, including without limitation music, and shall indemnify the copyright owners of the play(s) and their licensing agent, Concord Theatricals Corp., against any costs, expenses, losses and liabilities arising from the use of such copyrighted third-party materials by licensees. For music, please contact the appropriate music licensing authority in your territory for the rights to any incidental music.

IMPORTANT BILLING AND CREDIT REQUIREMENTS

If you have obtained performance rights to this title, please refer to your licensing agreement for important billing and credit requirements.

THE SWEARING JAR was first produced at the Toronto Fringe Festival (Toronto, Canada), with direction by Geoffrey Pounsett, in 2008 with the following cast:

CAREY . . . . Janet Porter
SIMON . . . . Andrew Pifko
OWEN . . . . Christopher Stanton
BEV . . . . Kyra Harper

The play had its U.S. premiere at the Bridge Theatre Company (New York), with direction by Rosemary Andress, in 2010 with the following cast:

CAREY . . . . Kate Hewlett
SIMON . . . . Vince Nappo
OWEN . . . . Christopher Stanton
BEV . . . . Mimi Quillan

The play had its professional premiere at Prairie Theatre Exchange in Winnipeg, Manitoba, with direction by Stewart Arnott, on November 12, 2012 with the following cast:

CAREY . . . . Sarah Constible
SIMON . . . . Gabriel Gosselin
OWEN . . . . Christopher Stanton
BEV . . . . Terri Cherniak

CHARACTERS

CAREY – mid-30s

SIMON – Carey's husband, late-30s

OWEN – guitar player, 20s-30s

BEV – Simon's mother, 60s-70s

SETTING

The play takes place in four locations: a small concert venue, the living room of Simon and Carey's house, a park, and a bookstore.

TIME

Present day.

AUTHOR'S NOTES

Having seen (or acted in!) a number of different productions of *The Swearing Jar*, I wanted to offer some gentle suggestions about rhythm and tone. With the exception of Bev, the characters speak before they think, so the dialogue should, for the most part, be fast-paced and rapid fire. That said, when the punctuation or stage directions call for silence, do not be afraid to live in these silences or at least explore them in rehearsal. As for tone...the production can fall flat when the first half is played for laughs, because the audience feels betrayed when the story turns. They feel they have ordered a comedy and been force-fed a tragedy! If, however, the tone is real and consistent throughout, the humor and pathos will both be allowed to breathe. Last note: all caps means the dialogue is ODDLY LOUD! Give it a shot and then pull back if it's too weird.

Quick note on casting: if the actor playing Simon is not particularly tall, feel free to change the lyrics of "Too Tall" to "Too Smart" and change "gentle giant" to "mental giant."

SONGS

"Too Tall" .... Carey

"The Night We Fought" .... Carey

"The Way to a Man's Heart" ....Owen & Carey

"You" .... Carey

"May the Fourth" ....Owen & Carey

"Family" .... Carey

"Forgetting Your Face" ....Owen & Carey

"The Turtle" .... Carey

Owen plays guitar on all songs.

Scene One

(The concert.)

*(**OWEN** sits on a stool tuning his guitar as the audience files in. He peers backstage then looks up at the booth and shrugs.)*

*(After the last audience member has been seated, a quiet knocking begins at the back of the house. **OWEN** does not hear it.)*

*(The house lights go down and a special comes up on **OWEN**.)*

OWEN. *(To the booth.)* We're...uh...we're not quite ready yet.

> *(The knocking escalates and the house lights come up again.)*

Can someone...?

> *(He gestures for an audience member to open the door. When some kind soul hopefully does, **CAREY** bursts in.)*

> *(She makes her way through the audience, greeting people as she passes them. When she reaches the stage, **OWEN** helps her up.)*

CAREY. *(Whispering to **OWEN**.)* The door was –

OWEN. Yep.

CAREY. *(To the audience.)* Thank you so much for joining us tonight to celebrate Simon's birthday. It means a lot to have you all together in one –

(She digs for something in her pocket, but finds nothing. She checks the other pocket.)

Shit. *(Realizing she has sworn.)* Shit! Shoot. Wow, maybe it's a good thing my mother-in-law decided not to –

(She spots **BEV** *in the audience.)*

Bev! You came. You look great. *(To* **OWEN**.*)* Where were we?

OWEN. You were swearing.

CAREY. Before that.

OWEN. You were looking for this?

(He holds up a piece of paper. **CAREY** *takes it.)*

CAREY. We're going to begin this evening with the first –

(She turns to **OWEN**.*)*

Thank you. For the –

(He nods.)

I'm going to begin with the first song I ever wrote for Simon. It's called "Too Tall."

[MUSIC NO. 01 "TOO TALL"]

*(***OWEN*** begins to play.* **CAREY** *takes a deep breath, then sings along.)*

I AWKWARDLY SMILED
YOU AWK –

(She cuts herself off and addresses the audience again.)

I should just say – I wrote this after a few martinis. So this is more like the fantasy version of our first date.

(**OWEN** *starts playing from the beginning again.*)

Which isn't that far off from what actually happened, except that in reality we slept together on the first –

(**OWEN** *plays as loudly as possible, trying to save her. She nods, then sings.*)

I AWKWARDLY SMILED
YOU AWKWARDLY KNEW
THAT I WOULD BE YOURS ONE DAY
AND YOU CAME OUT AND TOLD ME THAT TOO
AND YOU'RE AWFULLY TALL
I THOUGHT
AND MUCH TOO STUBBORN FOR ME
BUT SOMEHOW I WANT
I THOUGHT
NEED
I THOUGHT
LUST
FOR CONVERSATION WITH YOU
AWKWARD ME
MEETS WITTY YOU
DOES HER BEST TO PLAY IT COOL
AWKWARD GIRL
MEETS GENTLE GIANT
CAREFUL NOT TO BE RELIANT

YOU AWKWARDLY WATCHED
I AWKWARDLY CHEWED
AND ASKED YOU 'BOUT ALL YOUR GOALS
ALL THE THINGS THAT YOU WANTED TO DO
MY FACE SHOWED NO SIGN
BUT STILL YOUR FACE KNEW
THAT SIX SHORT MONTHS LATER
MY TOO TALL LOVE
I'D BE MARRIED TO YOU

Scene Two

(A memory.)

(Simon and Carey's living room.)

*(**CAREY** sits on the couch, mesmerized by a mop that's lying in front of her.)*

*(**SIMON** enters slowly, cautiously, wearing a tweed jacket and jeans. He is holding a yellow piece of paper.)*

*(He looks up at **CAREY**. Looks at the mop. Looks back at **CAREY**.)*

SIMON. Whatcha doin', honey?

CAREY. *(Still fixated on the mop.)* "Nurturing my weaknesses."

SIMON. And telekinesis is first on the list?

CAREY. Cleaning, you weirdo.

SIMON. I'm glad you're in my life, you know that?

*(**CAREY** gives him a suspicious look.)*

CAREY. Did you back over my bike with your car?

SIMON. No. I'm just feeling...grateful.

CAREY. Good. You're about to get grateful-er.

SIMON. Gratefuller is not a –

*(**CAREY** gestures for him to stop talking.)*

CAREY. I have some news.

SIMON. So do I.

(She notices his suit.)

CAREY. You look dapper.

SIMON. Well that's not news.

CAREY. Were you at a funeral?

SIMON. No, I told you. I had a photo shoot before my – "dapper." Thank you. It's itchy, though. I think I'm allergic to tweed.

CAREY. Yeah, you've said. Can you remind me to buy a new toothbrush? Mine fell in the toilet.

SIMON. Does your news by any chance involve Ritalin?

CAREY. Nope. It involves eggs.

SIMON. Disappointing.

CAREY. And your penis.

SIMON. Intriguing.

CAREY. And getting something cute and fuzzy that you've wanted for a long time.

> *(He folds up the yellow piece of paper and tucks it into his jacket pocket.* **CAREY** *notices.)*

What's that?

SIMON. You're getting my hopes up and if you are talking about a bunny, I will never forgive you.

CAREY. What does your penis have to do with a b – ?

SIMON. Carey.

> *(Silence. She studies his face. Smiles.)*

CAREY. Get excited.

SIMON. Holy sh –

CAREY. No! No more swearing. We have to be role models from now on. Well-rounded role models who mop.

SIMON. HOLY SHIT WE'RE HAVING A FUCKIN' BABY!! This isn't a joke, right?

CAREY. That would be mean.

SIMON. You've done that kind of thing before.

CAREY. Never again. No swearing, no dirty floors, no unmotivated cruelty.

(*He runs over to her, picks her up and spins her around.*)

SIMON. HOLY FRICKIN' POOP!!!

CAREY. I FRICKIN' KNOW, RIGHT?!!

(**SIMON** *puts her down and heads for the front door.*)

Where are you going?!

SIMON. I NEED SOME AIR!!

CAREY. Right now? Hey...hey! You can't tell people yet. Wait!

(*He stops.*)

What's yours?

SIMON. My what?

CAREY. Your news.

SIMON. It pales in comparison.

CAREY. I thought it might.

(*He kisses her quickly then exits.* **CAREY** *watches him go.*)

(*Under her breath.*) Holy shit.

Scene Three

(The concert.)

[MUSIC NO. 02 "THE NIGHT WE FOUGHT"]

*(**CAREY** sings a rousing drinking song. **OWEN** accompanies her on guitar.)*

CAREY.

THE NIGHT WE FOUGHT I TOLD YOU THAT I HATED KIDS
THE NIGHT WE FOUGHT YOU LIED THAT YOU DID TOO
BUT WHEN I LAY BESIDE YOU WITH MY HAND ON YOURS
I KNEW I WANTED KIDS WITH ONLY YOU
YOU WERE SULKING
AND I KNEW I WANTED KIDS WITH ONLY YOU
THE NIGHT YOU GOT SO DRUNK YOU WON YOUR POKER
    GAME
I TUCKED YOU IN AND WATCHED YOU WHILE YOU
    SNORED
AND THOUGH I'D ALWAYS THOUGHT LOVE WAS A
    FANTASY
THAT'S 'CAUSE I'D NEVER BEEN IN LOVE BEFORE
YOU WERE DROOLING
AND I'D NEVER BEEN IN LOVE LIKE THIS BEFORE

CAREY & OWEN.

OH...

CAREY.

WHETHER IT'S RIGHT OR WRETCHED

CAREY & OWEN.

DON'T GO

CAREY.

BABY LET'S MAKE THIS ONE NIGHT STAND
YOU WON WHAT YOU CAME FOR
THE GIRL WHO YOU WANTED TO LAND
WITHOUT PLAYING A HAND

SO ON THIS NIGHT I'M TELLING YOU I'M YOURS FOR LIFE
AND ON THIS NIGHT I KNOW YOU FEEL IT TOO
AND ONE DAY WHEN WE'RE OLD AND GREY AND HAVE
    TEN KIDS
WE'LL LAUGH ABOUT THE THINGS WE THOUGHT WE
    KNEW

Scene Four

(A memory.)

(Simon and Carey's living room.)

*(**CAREY** is sprawled out on the floor flipping through baby books. **SIMON** sits on the couch reading a newspaper.)*

CAREY. Jamar. James. Jasper?

SIMON. *Jesus.*

CAREY. I think it's too recognizable.

*(**SIMON** gives her joke a thumbs-down.)*

You're super grumpy today.

SIMON. Thanks for saying so. Always helps.

CAREY. "Jesus" counts as a swear word, by the way. That's five bucks in the cursing jar.

SIMON. If there's a cursing jar – and just as an aside, no one under the age of eighty uses the word "cursing" anymore – it isn't activated until both parties are aware of its existence. Also, five dollars is too much. Last time it was five cents.

CAREY. Honey?

SIMON. Yes, Love Muffin?

CAREY. Why are you reading the obituaries?

SIMON. I'm being a responsible husband and looking up baby names.

CAREY. Simon, they're dead people.

SIMON. It's shocking to me that people have to go through life with some of these names. Eleanor Fartz, for example.

CAREY. That is not in there.

SIMON. It is! "Eleanor Fartz." What kind of life must she have had with that name?

CAREY. Was she married?

SIMON. Um...da da da...yada yada... "loving wife to Lewis." Yep.

CAREY. Lewis Fartz. Wow. And she took his name.

(*She squints at the newspaper over his shoulder.*)

Oh, it's Fartz with a zed.

SIMON. Zee.

CAREY. Zed, you freak.

SIMON. Anyway. What difference does the zee make?

CAREY. It's *Fartz*. Not *Farts*.

(**CAREY** *continues reading the obituary over his shoulder.*)

Aw, man, they had kids. Fucking car accidents.

(**SIMON** *looks around, searching for something. He picks up a mason jar full of flowers and dumps the contents into the garbage.*)

Hey!

(**SIMON** *holds out the empty jar.* **CAREY** *stares at it, then rolls her eyes.*)

SIMON. It's your rule.

CAREY. Fine.

(*She searches her pockets.*)

Can I borrow five dollars?

SIMON. Unbelievable.

> *(He takes a five-dollar-bill out of his pocket and drops it into the jar. He picks up the newspaper again.)*

How do you know it was a car accident?

CAREY. It says right there. "Died suddenly."

> *(****SIMON*** *stares at her blankly.)*

It's code for "car accident." Or "subway jumper." And I just can't believe that Ms. Fartz would take her own life.

> *(****SIMON*** *continues reading.)*

SIMON. Hey, look at this one: Monica Motherfucker.

> *(****CAREY*** *laughs and wrestles the newspaper away from him. She reads it.)*

CAREY. Oooh. "Lavinia." I like that. I'm gonna add that to my list.

> *(****SIMON*** *squints at her.)*

What.

SIMON. Lavinia is a character from a Shakespeare play.

CAREY. Perfect. It'll make us sound smart.

SIMON. She had her hands hacked off and her tongue cut out.

CAREY. And that, right there, is why I don't like Shakespeare.

SIMON. Stick to the comedies. Fewer amputations. "How happy some o'er other some can be; through Athens, I am thought as fair as she."

CAREY. Um...why do you know that?

SIMON. I trod the boards a few times in high school.

CAREY. That is a shameless lie.

SIMON. I never lie. I did *A Midsummer Night's Dream* in Grade 9, *The Winter's Tale* in Grade 10, and *A Midsummer Night's Dream* in Grade 11.

CAREY. Were you the donkey?

SIMON. I'll have you know that I won Holy Blessed Sacrament's Dramatic Arts Award for my portrayal of a young lover.

CAREY. I'm very proud of you. Why haven't you bragged about this before?

SIMON. *(Under his breath.)* Because I played Helena.

CAREY. Excuse me?

SIMON. I played Helena.

CAREY. You played –

SIMON. It was an all-boys school and I was skinny. With full lips and a demure disposition.

CAREY. Oh my god. Do another one.

SIMON. No.

CAREY. I'll let you win the next three fights.

SIMON. "And I, an old turtle, will – "

CAREY. You played a turtle too?

SIMON. It's from *The Winter's Tale*. It's a metaphor. "And I, an old turtle, will wing me to some wither'd – "

CAREY. Turtles can't fly.

SIMON. I believe Mr. Shakespeare is referring to a turtledove.

CAREY. Then why doesn't he just –

SIMON. "AND I, AN OLD TURTLE, will wing me to some wither'd bough; And there my mate that's never to be found again, lament 'til I am lost."

(He bows. An odd silence.)

CAREY. Okay, that's enough couple time.

(She gets up.)

I like that one. Write that down for me.

SIMON. Aha! A born-again fan of The Bard. Where are you going?

CAREY. I need to wing me to school where thirty-six young minds are waiting to be shaped.

SIMON. I wasn't aware that Grade 7 Band could shape minds.

(CAREY gives him the finger and heads for the door.)

Wait. I want to give you something.

CAREY. No.

SIMON. Please?

CAREY. Nope.

SIMON. I'm not going to do anything.

CAREY. I don't trust you even a little bit.

SIMON. C'mere...

(CAREY approaches him in stages, hesitantly. When she reaches the couch, SIMON kisses her.)

CAREY. What was that for?

SIMON. I haven't kissed you in a while.

CAREY. You kissed me this m –

SIMON. Shhhh.

> (**CAREY** *runs her fingers through* **SIMON***'s hair and peers over his shoulder at the newspaper.*)

CAREY. Why can't you read the funnies like a normal person?

SIMON. Must all of your vocabulary come from *The Golden Girls*?

> (*She holds up the newspaper.*)

CAREY. This is depressing. Don't be depressing.

> (*She picks up one of Simon's books from the coffee table and turns to the back cover.*)

Be this guy.

SIMON. You know that's me, right?

CAREY. Look how happy you are. With your big white teeth.

SIMON. The better to eat you with.

CAREY. Ew.

SIMON. No...

CAREY. I'm leaving you. Think about names.

> (**SIMON** *gives her an exaggerated, toothy smile.*)

SIMON. Yes deeeear.

Scene Five

(A memory.)

(A bookstore.)

*(**CAREY** stands in the aisle studying the back cover of Simon's book. **OWEN**, wearing khaki pants and a denim shirt, approaches **CAREY** and looks over her shoulder at the book. He points to the picture of Simon.)*

OWEN. I love that writer.

CAREY. Yeah, me too.

OWEN. Can I help you with anything?

CAREY. I'm fine thanks. Just browsing.

OWEN. Okay.

(He turns to leave.)

CAREY. I don't know why I do that.

OWEN. Excuse me?

CAREY. I always do that. I panic when someone asks if I need help. Yes, I need help. I NEED HELP!

(Silence.)

I am actually fine, though. In this particular situation.

OWEN. Okay.

*(He leaves. **CAREY** puts Simon's book back on the shelf. She sits on the floor then takes a napkin and pen out of her purse. After a few moments, the pen runs out of ink. She shakes it. Nothing. She wets the end. Still nothing.)*

*(**OWEN** approaches her again.)*

Do you need a pen?

CAREY. I do, thanks.

    (He searches his pockets.)

OWEN. I...don't have one.

    (He takes off, then returns with a pen. **CAREY** *takes it, amused.)*

OWEN. What are you writing?

CAREY. Lyrics, sort of.

OWEN. You write songs!

CAREY. I do. Once every seventeen years or so.

OWEN. What have you got so far, if you don't mind my asking?

CAREY. Of...my...?

OWEN. If you don't mind my asking.

CAREY. "May the Fourth."

OWEN. The date.

CAREY. But also the title.

OWEN. Well, I have a good feeling about it.

CAREY. Thank you.

OWEN. May the Fourth be with you.

CAREY. No.

OWEN. I'm Owen, by the way.

CAREY. Hi, Owen.

    (They shake hands.)

OWEN. Do you always write songs in bookstores?

CAREY. Nah, it's been a weird day.

OWEN. I'm sorry to hear that.

CAREY. Not bad weird, just...yeah no it was bad weird.

OWEN. Can I help you?

CAREY. With my day?

OWEN. With anything. With your day, with listening, with –

> (OWEN *points directly at* CAREY's *chest. She looks down, alarmed.*)

You have –

CAREY. Um...

OWEN. A crumb! Maybe from a piece of cake. Or a cookie of some kind.

CAREY. Probably. There are a lot of cookies in my life these days.

OWEN. Do you work in a –

CAREY. Nope.

> (*A very long silence.*)

OWEN. I'm sorry. I'm not so good with –

CAREY. Small talk?

OWEN. Gorgeous people. People I find gorgeous. I'm in a band!

> (CAREY *laughs.*)

I just mean, this isn't what I do. Working here. I mean, I do work here, but it's not who I am. Not that I judge people who *do* do just this. Do you need help finding a book?

CAREY. Yes.

OWEN. Great. I'm sweating.

CAREY. I woke up this morning and decided that today was the day. To make some changes.

OWEN. Sounds very healthy.

CAREY. Starting with a new hobby.

OWEN. Any particular kind of hobby?

CAREY. I was thinking of doing some painting. Pictures, not houses.

OWEN. You're an artist *and* a musician?

CAREY. God no. I can't even draw a happy face. I just thought it would be good to have a creative outlet.

OWEN. Other than music.

CAREY. Yes.

OWEN. Why don't you just get better at music?

CAREY. Thanks.

OWEN. No it's just – I took French in high school, then Spanish and German in university, then Italian and Korean last year when I broke my patella.

CAREY. You speak...six languages?

OWEN. I speak no languages. That's exactly my point. If I had stuck with French, I could be the Prime Minister right now. Or the Premier Ministre.

> *(He laughs.)*

Instead, I'm slinging books in khaki pants. Do you play guitar?

CAREY. I used to but I quit. I'm more of a singer. Well, I used to be. It's been a while since... I don't really – . It's a long story.

OWEN. I've got time.

CAREY. Don't you have customers?

OWEN. Screw 'em. You wanna grab a coffee?

CAREY. I can't.

OWEN. Of course.

CAREY. I would love to.

OWEN. But...

CAREY. Can't.

   (A beat.)

CAREY.   **OWEN.**
   Anyway, I'd better –   You haven't told me your –

CAREY. It was nice to meet you, Owen.

   *(She exits. **OWEN** watches her go then returns
   to his work. After a few beats, **CAREY** runs
   back in. She hands him her business card.)*

I'm – me. That's me.

   *(She shrugs and hurries out again. **OWEN**
   studies the card, smitten.)*

Scene Six

(A memory.)

(Simon and Carey's living room.)

*(**CAREY** sits on the couch figuring out the lyrics to a new song. **SIMON** enters and watches her.)*

CAREY.

"YOU, YOU CAME ALONG..."

(She scribbles down some lyrics.)

"AND YOU FOUND YOUR WAY TO ME, THROUGH THAT DEEP BULLSHIT SEA..."

*(**SIMON** goes and gets the swearing jar.)*

"...from which I'd been drinking." *(To herself)* No. Too gross.

"IN WHICH I'D BEEN DROWNING."

Better.

"YOU TOOK, MY –"

*(**SIMON** holds out the jar. **CAREY** looks up at him.)*

What.

SIMON. You said "bullshit."

CAREY. No I didn't.

SIMON. You sang it.

CAREY. Sing-swearing doesn't count.

SIMON. Really?

CAREY. Mm-hm.

SIMON. *(Fake-singing.)*
"I WISH YOU HAD FUCKIN' TOLD ME THAT, YOU A-ASS-HOLE, BECAUSE I REALLY – "

(CAREY takes the jar.)

What are we going to use all that cash for, anyway?

CAREY. The baby.

SIMON. That's so boring.

CAREY. Simon!

SIMON. We should save for a vacation in Cuba or something.

CAREY. Yes, because communism is so relaxing.

SIMON. North Korea?

CAREY. I hate to burst your bubble, but we aren't going to be taking a vacation until the little peanut is in school. Which means at least three years.

SIMON. We should do it sooner than that.

CAREY. Oh my god, you'll be forty!

SIMON. I will not!

CAREY. You will!

SIMON. I will not be forty. I will never be forty.

(He considers this.)

Forty sucks.

CAREY. That's what we're saving for. A big, fat, fortieth birthday party. With forty big fat candles on your forty-inch cake.

SIMON. *(Resuming fake-singing.)*
"WHY YOU GOTTA BEEE SUCH A DICK. A DICKY LITTLE DICK WITH A BABY IN HER B – "

(The doorbell rings.)

CAREY. That'll be your new wife.

SIMON. Ooooh, I hope she has nice boobs.

> *(**SIMON** goes to the door and opens it to reveal his mother, **BEV**, with an unlit cigarette in her mouth.)*

Ew.

BEV. Well that's a nice greeting.

> *(**CAREY** heads over to **BEV** and kisses her on the cheek.)*

CAREY. Hi, Bev. Come on in.

SIMON. I hope you weren't smoking on our lawn.

BEV. I wasn't smoking. I was quitting.

SIMON. With a cigarette in your mouth?

BEV. An unlit menthol cigarette, yes. This is Phase Two.

CAREY. What was Phase One?

BEV. Phase One was switching to menthols.

SIMON. You've always smoked menthols.

BEV. Phase One is a very long phase.

> *(**BEV** takes a seat on the couch. She looks at **SIMON**, then at **CAREY**.)*

So?

CAREY. Um…

BEV. Why am I here?

CAREY. Beee…cause you missed us?

BEV. Simon left me a message.

CAREY. *(To **SIMON**.)* He did?

SIMON. And you didn't think to maybe phone back?

BEV. I've been trying you for days.

> (BEV *shifts her focus to* CAREY.)

"I need to talk to you about something, Mother. I have some important news."

> (BEV *clucks disapprovingly.*)

"Mother."

CAREY. Well that's interesting, because I can't think of anything he'd need to tell you. Especially not now. *(Glaring at* SIMON.*)* This month.

BEV. What's the news?

CAREY. Yes, Simon, what's the news?

SIMON. The news...is...that...we have decided to get some help.

BEV. Like a maid? I'll call the papers.

SIMON. With baby-making.

BEV. That sounds illegal.

SIMON. Yes, mother, we've hired a team of male hookers to –

CAREY. What Simon means is that we've decided to start *trying* to have a baby. So hopefully, if all goes well, we'll get some actual news sometime soon and then we can *wait until the first trimester is over* and let you know. Right, Simon?

> (SIMON *looks back and forth between his mother and his wife.*)

SIMON. WE'RE HAVING A BABY!

CAREY. Simon!

BEV. Oh my lord.

SIMON. I know!

BEV. Are you sure?

SIMON. Yes, Mom. You're going to be a g –

BEV. Don't you dare.

> (**BEV** *looks at* **CAREY**, *then starts bouncing a little.*)

A baby!

CAREY. I'm only at ten weeks. Well, nine and a half weeks.

SIMON. So different from the movie.

BEV. Baby baby baby!

> (**BEV** *and* **SIMON** *start jumping up and down.*)

CAREY. Please try to keep this to yourself.

BEV. I am as silent as the grave.

SIMON. And just as warm.

CAREY. It actually feels good to tell someone.

> (**SIMON** *bounces over to* **CAREY**.)

Just because I'm not frowning doesn't mean you're not in serious trouble.

SIMON. Didn't understand that. Too many negatives. Gonna keep jumping.

> (*He bounces away from her again.*)

BEV. You need to work on how you deliver good news. That message was positively somber.

> (**BEV** *gives* **CAREY**'s *shoulders a strange little tap.*)

Well done. With the baby-making. You'll be a wonderful mother.

CAREY. Aww, that's –

BEV. And thank goodness, because if Simon's anything like his father, you'll be doing it all on your own.

SIMON. Excuse me?

BEV. What. He abandoned us. Those kinds of issues can be genetic.

SIMON. He didn't *abandon* us. He died.

BEV. *(To* CAREY.*)* He did that too.

SIMON. Well this is fun. You should invite yourself over more often.

BEV. Don't be so sensitive. I'm simply saying that –

SIMON. You just found out that we're having a baby! And these are the first words out of your mouth?

CAREY. Simon, it's fine. She's –

SIMON. *(Still on* BEV.*)* I'd rather be like him than like you.

CAREY. Simon!

BEV. And there it is.

>   (BEV *heads for the kitchen.)*

Excuse me.

CAREY. Bev, he didn't mean it.

SIMON. Yes he did.

BEV. I need a glass of water.

>   (BEV *exits to the kitchen.* CAREY *wheels around.)*

CAREY. What was *that*?

SIMON. You cannot possibly take her side on this one.

CAREY. I'm not taking anyone's side, because I'm an adult, not a six-year-old.

SIMON. She makes me want to kill people with my hands.

CAREY. Then why did you phone her?

SIMON. I didn't expect her to – can we just enjoy this moment? We're having a baby. And my mother actually smiled for four and a half seconds.

CAREY. You weren't supposed to tell anyone.

SIMON. I know. But look how handsome I am.

(He poses for her. **CAREY** *fights a smile.)*

CAREY. Go in there and make her feel better. Then come back out here and make me feel better.

SIMON. Can I use my magic sex pinkies?

CAREY. Not this time.

(He scowls and exits to the kitchen.)

Scene Seven

(The concert.)

[MUSIC NO. 03 "THE WAY TO A MAN'S HEART"]

*(**OWEN** rocks out on the guitar. **CAREY** joins him, singing.)*

CAREY.
THE WAY TO A MAN'S HEART IS RIGHT THROUGH HIS
STOMACH
THE WAY TO MY HEART'S THROUGH MY CHEST
AND YOU, ONLY YOU, KNOW THE WAY TO MY HEART
SO YOU PULL BACK THE SKIN AND YOU PRESS
AND YOU HEAR THE CRACKING
AND YOU HEAR THE SNAPPING
AND YOU KEEP ON PUSHING UNTIL
YOU'VE FOUND WHAT YOU WANTED
YOUR HAND'S ON THE PRIZE
AND MY WARM BEATING HEART STARTS TO CHILL

CAREY & OWEN.
AND WE ARE ANGRY
WE ARE FIGHTING
WE ARE LOVING HARD
AND YOU STAY WITH ME
WHEN I'M ANGRY
SO KEEP IT, KEEP MY HEART

CAREY.
THE WAY TO A MAN'S HEART IS RIGHT THROUGH HIS
STOMACH
THE WAY TO YOUR HEART'S THROUGH YOUR MIND
IT'S SHARPER THAN MINE IS
IT'S CRUELER THAN MINE IS
ITS DEFAULT IS WITTY, NOT KIND

WE FIGHT AND WE FALL
WE GET DRUNK, WE GET SMALL
AND IT'S NOT EVEN NOON WHEN WE'RE DONE
I CANNOT PUSH YOU IN
'CAUSE I KNOW YOU CAN'T SWIM
BUT YOU CANNOT CONTEST THAT I'VE WON

CAREY & OWEN.

AND I AM HOLDING
OUT YOUR HEART NOW
AND I NEVER KNEW
THAT IT WAS WITH ME
ALL THIS TIME
I KEPT IT SAFE FOR YOU

OWEN.

WE FIGHT AND WE FALL
WE GET DRUNK WE GET
    SMALL
AND IT'S NOT EVEN NOON
WHEN WE'RE DONE
I CANNOT PUSH YOU IN
I KNOW YOU CAN'T SWIM
YOU CANNOT CONTEST
THAT I'VE WON

CAREY.

OH I AM HOLDING
OUT YOUR HEART NOW

AND I NEVER KNEW

THAT IT WAS WITH ME
ALL THIS TIME
I KEPT IT SAFE
FOR YOU

Scene Eight

(A memory.)

(The bookstore.)

*(**CAREY** approaches **OWEN** and taps him on the back. **OWEN** jumps.)*

OWEN. Jesus Fuck!

CAREY. Sorry. I'm so sorry.

OWEN. No, my upper back is just really sensitive and I didn't hear you coming. Didn't see ya there! You look nice today.

CAREY. Thanks. *(A beat.)* Did I look a little rough last time?

OWEN. No, just tired.

CAREY. Wow. Well, Owen, you look nice today too.

OWEN. *(Studying his pants.)* They make us wear these.

(An awkward silence.)

CAREY. I'm Carey, by the way. I don't think I actually told you that last time.

OWEN. It was on your business card.

CAREY. Right.

OWEN. Which you gave to me.

CAREY. I remember.

OWEN. And to which I responded in the form of an email. Twice.

CAREY. I...remember.

OWEN. Why didn't you write back?

CAREY. I was trapped under something heavy? Twice?

> (**CAREY** *laughs.* **OWEN** *does not.*)

I shouldn't have done that, the other day. Given you my – I'm going through a bit of a rough patch and I – I don't know what came over me. I'm not in any position to be – that is to say, I'm – I have a…things are a bit complicated. Right now.

OWEN. Why?

CAREY. I'm a serial killer?

OWEN. No.

CAREY. I'm seriously not allowed to make jokes?

OWEN. Why are things complicated?

CAREY. I can't go on dates and I shouldn't be giving out my phone number.

OWEN. Why not?

CAREY. I have a situation.

OWEN. A situation.

CAREY. Yep.

OWEN. You're taken?

CAREY. I'm not "taken," I'm – that's a weird way of – "taken." I'm not that.

OWEN. Do you like me?

CAREY. I thought I did. But these questions are…

OWEN. Go on a date with me.

CAREY. I can't.

OWEN. Go for a walk with me?

CAREY. Okay.

OWEN. Okay.

(He moves to leave.)

CAREY. What. Now?

OWEN. Why not?

CAREY. You're working.

OWEN. I hate this job. Come with me.

(He offers her his arm. She doesn't take it.)

CAREY. I'm not leaving this store with you.

OWEN. Please.

CAREY. Not in those pants. You'll get beaten up.

*(**OWEN** smiles.)*

OWEN. Fine.

*(**OWEN** starts unbutton his shirt. **CAREY** laughs, stopping him. He offers his arm again and she takes it.)*

Scene Nine

(The concert.)

(CAREY steps forward and addresses the audience.)

CAREY. Marriage can be hard work, as many of you know. *(She gestures to a couple in the audience.)* We all – *(She stops herself and turns back to the couple.)* I didn't mean you two in particular, obviously. You seem very –

(Returning to her speech.)

We all do stupid things and we all make mistakes. Sometimes very big ones. But when you are wildly in love, you find a way to move past these mistakes. Because it is a "rare and miraculous thing...

(Smiling at a specific person in the audience.)

"...to find your one, true soul mate."

[MUSIC NO. 04 "YOU"]

(OWEN plays. She sings.)

YOU
YOU CAME ALONG –

(OWEN stops playing. CAREY turns to face him.)

Whoops. Ready?

(OWEN nods. There is a sense of tension between them. He begins to play again. CAREY sings.)

YOU
YOU CAME ALONG

AND YOU FOUND YOUR WAY TO ME
THROUGH ALL THE MYSTERY
I THOUGHT I HAD
AND YOU
YOU LOUDMOUTH, YOU
YOU TALK AT THE SAME TIME AS ME
BUT THAT DOESN'T GUARANTEE
THAT YOU'RE NOT LIST'NING

>   (**CAREY** *moves closer to* **OWEN**. *He turns
>   away slightly. She notices.*)

BEFORE YOU, LOVE WAS A KICK IN THE TEETH
'CAUSE MOST MEN WERE SCARED AND THE OTHERS WERE
    CHEAP
BUT YOU WEREN'T SCARED TO BE MINE
TO BE KIND
AND YOU –

>   (**OWEN** *plays the wrong part of the song.*)

OWEN. Oh right, it goes back to the – ok.

>   (*He begins to play again.* **CAREY** *tries to catch
>   his eye but he won't engage. They are a bit out
>   of sync at first, but they find their groove.*)

AND YOU
YOU CAME ALONG
YOU DOG-PADDLED YOUR WAY TO ME
THROUGH THAT DEEP DIRTY SEA
IN WHICH I'D BEEN DROWNING
YOU TOOK
MY CAUTIOUS HAND
AND YOU ASKED ME TO BE YOUR WIFE
SWIM TOGETHER AND BUILD A LIFE
CHOKE ON LAUGHTER TOGETHER
AND I THOUGHT LOVE WAS LIKE SICKNESS AND DEATH

YOU KNOW THEY'RE COMING BUT YOU DON'T HOLD YOUR
    BREATH
BUT I DID NOT KNOW A TENTH
OF LOVE'S STRENGTH
UNTIL YOU
UNTIL YOU
UNTIL YOU, YOU –

> (**OWEN** *plays the wrong chord again.* **CAREY**
> *looks at him.*)

– WENT AWAY

I don't know how to play this one.

CAREY. Okay, we'll just – we'll move on to the next part.

Scene Ten

(A memory.)

(Simon and Carey's living room. They are mid-argument.)

CAREY. Episiotomy. Placenta. Push, Carey, push. These things do not excite me, okay?

SIMON. Carey...

CAREY. Loss of bowel control, ripping of any kind. Do you understand what I am saying? I CANNOT HAVE A BABY. I don't even like children.

SIMON. You're a *teacher*.

CAREY. Exactly! So I know. They're manipulative and they're too stupid to even hide it. They're us, but worse. Why would I want to go through all that pain and... and...puffiness, just so that I can bring a bald, mini version of myself into this world and teach it all the things that are wrong with us, plus new things. NO THANKS.

SIMON. CAREY!

CAREY. WHAT?!

SIMON. I have a headache. And you're ranting.

CAREY. You always have a headache. And *you're* ranting.

(A beat.)

I don't want a baby.

SIMON. Yes you do.

CAREY. Don't tell me what I want. Haven't you ever heard of freedom of choice?

SIMON. You've been taking prenatal vitamins since we met.

CAREY. Because they're gummies and they're delicious!

SIMON. You told me you wanted this.

CAREY. I know!

SIMON. So what is going on? And why is it going on SO FUCKING LOUDLY?

(**CAREY** *picks up the jar and holds it out.*)

NOT RIGHT NOW!

(**CAREY** *lowers the jar.*)

CAREY. Are you okay?

SIMON. Me? You're the one turning into Satan's evil wife.

CAREY. Wouldn't that make you Satan?

SIMON. Carey.

(**CAREY** *takes a deep breath.* **SIMON** *sits down on the couch.*)

CAREY. Ever since I told you about the baby, you've been weird.

SIMON. What?

CAREY. If it's going to change everything –

SIMON. Are we honestly having this conversation?

CAREY. Maybe we aren't ready.

SIMON. We've been "ready" for years.

CAREY. I know! I just – I don't want to feel like I'm doing this all by myself.

SIMON. You're not.

(*A beat.*)

You could, though.

CAREY. What?

SIMON. Do it by yourself. If you had to. So could I.

(**CAREY** *tosses the jar at him.*)

SIMON. Ow!

CAREY. You see?! That's the kind of stuff I'm talking about. Who says that to their pregnant wife?

SIMON. I have never wanted anything this much in my entire life.

CAREY. So why are you being weird?

SIMON. I'm not being – tell me how I'm being weird.

CAREY. You slept on your stomach instead of your back.

SIMON. What?!

CAREY. And you're not maintaining eye contact.

SIMON. Is it...*possible*...that this is hormonal?

CAREY. Is it *possible*...

(*She goes and gets a five-dollar bill from her purse.*)

...that you are an assface?

(*She drops the bill into the jar.*)

Are. You. Okay.

(*A long, heavy silence. He looks up at her.*)

SIMON. No.

CAREY. Oh my god oh my god oh my god.

SIMON. Whoa, whoooaaa, I just meant that –

CAREY. What is it? Are – do you hate me? Are you cheating on me? Are you sick?

(**CAREY** *gets a pain in her stomach and winces.*)

SIMON. Hey, what's going on?

CAREY. I just have a cramp, okay? I've been getting cramps. Why aren't you okay?

SIMON. I...I just meant...that I could never be described as "okay." I am exquisite. A Greek god with the intellect of a –

CAREY. You were joking? That was a joke?

SIMON. I was trying to lighten the mood. In retrospect, it may have been the wrong choice.

(**CAREY** *picks up the jar.*)

Can you please sit down? I do not want you to get stressed out and give birth to a walnut-sized baby right now.

CAREY. Swear to me.

SIMON. "Fuckballs."

CAREY. Nothing about this is funny. Swear to me that everything's okay. That we're gonna be okay.

SIMON. Oh my god. I swear.

(**CAREY** *holds out the jar.*)

CAREY. Make it official.

SIMON. It's a totally different kind of swearing!

(**CAREY** *doesn't budge.*)

I, Simon Patterson, swear that everything is okay.

(*He searches his pockets for cash. Finding nothing, he drops his credit card into the jar.*)

CAREY. Expand.

SIMON. I swear that I do not hate you, I am not cheating on you, I'm not... I'm fine, we're fine. You're *insane*, but we're fine.

CAREY. I didn't want babies. But then I did, and now that I'm having one, if you leave me... I will track you down and I will kill you.

SIMON. And I will support that decision.

CAREY. We can get through anything. You know that, right? We just have to be in it together.

SIMON. I'm sorry I scared you. That conversation...got away from me.

> (CAREY *hugs* SIMON, *then cups his face in her hands, making eye contact with him. They stay like this for a long time, their eyes locked.* SIMON *is the first to break eye contact.*)

CAREY. *(Quietly.)* See?

> (*Frustrated,* SIMON *moves her hands off his face then turns away.*)

Scene Eleven

(The concert.)

[MUSIC NO. 05 "MAY THE FOURTH"]

*(**OWEN** plays and sings.)*

OWEN.
>EV'RY TIME I LEAVE
>I THINK OF ALL THE TIMES BEFORE THIS
>WAVING CASU'LLY
>DOESN'T MATTER IF YOU NOTICE

CAREY & OWEN.
>MAY THE FOURTH IS HERE
>FASTER THAN IN YEARS BEFORE THIS
>MY MISTAKES ARE CLEAR
>BUT YOU'RE TOO FAR AWAY TO NOTICE
>AND I TAKE ALL OF YOU FOR GRANTED
>EV'RY PART THAT I IGNORE
>AND IF I TELL YOU HOW I LOVE YOU
>I WILL LOSE MYSELF FOR SURE

CAREY.
>SO EV'RY TIME I LEAVE
>IT FEELS AS THOUGH I'VE LEFT FOREVER
>YOUR HEART IS ON YOUR SLEEVE
>BUT MINE STAYS DRY IN RAINY WEATHER

CAREY & OWEN.
>AND I TAKE ALL OF YOU FOR GRANTED
>EV'RY PART THAT I IGNORE

>*(**OWEN** harmonizes somewhat freely.)*

>AND IF YOU TELL ME ONLY TRUTH NOW
>I WILL LOSE MYSELF FOR SURE

>*(**OWEN** hums.)*

CAREY & OWEN.

  BUT EVERY TIME I LEAVE

  YOU WAIT PEACEFULLY

  YOU WAIT PEACEFULLY

CAREY.

  YOU WAIT PEACEFULLY

Scene Twelve

(A memory.)

(The park. Afternoon. **OWEN** *and* **CAREY** *sit in the grass side by side. His guitar lies next to them.)*

*(***OWEN*** *takes out a bottle of wine and holds it up.)*

CAREY. I really shouldn't drink in public. I have bad luck with cops.

OWEN. Thank god someone invented the Thermos.

(He pours her wine into a thermos.)

CAREY. I guess one won't kill me.

OWEN. Can I ask you a question?

CAREY. Yep.

OWEN. Okay, I just have to think of one...

*(***CAREY*** *laughs.)*

Do you want kids?

CAREY. Yikes. That's a bigger –

OWEN. Do you snore?

CAREY. I do not snore, but I sleepwalk. And occasionally sleep-punch.

OWEN. The first girl I ever dated gave me a black eye.

CAREY. In her sleep?

OWEN. Nope.

CAREY. So, how does that relate to –

OWEN. I was asleep.

CAREY. What did you do?

OWEN. I woke up.

CAREY. No, to deserve that.

OWEN. Nothing! She was aiming for the alarm clock and her depth perception was off. Your turn.

CAREY. Um...what do your parents do?

OWEN. They died.

CAREY. Oh no. I thought that would be a safe one.

OWEN. I don't mind talking about it. I'll talk about pretty much anything. Death, ex-girlfriends, musicals, anything.

> (**CAREY** studies his face.)

CAREY. You're honest, aren't you? You're a good person.

OWEN. This feels like a trap.

CAREY. 'Cause I'm not sure that I am. I feel guilty all the time. I just walk around feeling like I don't even deserve to –

> (She wells up. **OWEN** takes a handkerchief out of his pocket and offers it to her.)

OWEN. It's not dirty. It just needs to be ironed.

CAREY. You were born in the wrong century.

OWEN. I think so too. I much prefer horses to cars, for example.

> (He dries her eyes for her, then puts the handkerchief back in his pocket. They stare at each other.)

I've been thinking about you. Quite a lot, actually. Not a creepy amount, but I was hoping that...well, I think you're... I find you to be...

(He clears his throat.)

I get very nervous. I don't know if it shows.

CAREY. Hardly at all.

OWEN. I'm happy that you're here, is what I'm trying to say.

(He leans in for a kiss. She balks.)

CAREY. Sorry.

OWEN. No, yeah, of course.

CAREY. You're great.

OWEN. I had to try. I figured it would feel worse not to.

(A beat.)

Turns out I was incorrect.

*(**CAREY** picks up Owen's guitar.)*

CAREY. Play something?

*(**OWEN** waits, then takes it from her. He starts to gently pluck the chords ad-libbing a mournful guitar song.)*

*(**CAREY** lies down on her side next to him, watching him.)*

*(**BEV** enters, smoking a cigarette. When she sees **CAREY**, she stops dead in her tracks.)*

*(Oblivious, **CAREY** rests her hand on **OWEN**'s knee. He continues playing, but he slows his tempo dramatically, distracted by the physical contact.)*

*(**CAREY** sits up and kisses **OWEN**. He stops playing.)*

> (**BEV** *tries to walk past them, but* **CAREY** *sees her and pulls away.*)

Hi!

BEV. Hello.

CAREY. I – how are you?

BEV. I've been better.

CAREY. Yes, are you –

BEV. I'm in a bit of a hurry, actually. My car. My – the parking meter.

CAREY. Of course.

> (**BEV** *looks at* **OWEN** *sadly. She nods a hello, then walks away.*)

OWEN. That was strange. Who was that?

> (*A beat.*)

Carey?

CAREY. (*Shaking her head.*) Our first kiss. That's perfect.

OWEN. Carey, who was that?

> (**CAREY** *starts packing up her things.*)

You okay?

CAREY. It was Simon's mother.

OWEN. Who's Simon?

CAREY. Please just leave it alone.

OWEN. Leave what? What am I –

CAREY. I just – I haven't seen her in a while.

OWEN. Carey, who's Simon?

CAREY. You're gonna push this? You really want to push this?

(A beat.)

My husband.

*(**OWEN** laughs. **CAREY** does not. As the realization sinks in, **OWEN**'s face falls.)*

*(**CAREY** exits, leaving him alone in the park.)*

Scene Thirteen

(A memory.)

(Simon and Carey's living room.)

*(**SIMON** is wearing a baseball cap and sunglasses. He is studying an ultrasound photo.)*

CAREY. I just ran into your mother.

SIMON. With your car?

CAREY. She looked like she'd been crying again.

SIMON. She's fine. I was just hitting her a little bit.

CAREY. *(Laughing.)* Seriously, I hope she's okay. She hasn't been herself lately.

SIMON. I know.

CAREY. So what's it about?

SIMON. I've – she's just been having a tough time with some things.

CAREY. Private things.

SIMON. Yeah.

CAREY. Okay. Well I hope you were sympathetic.

SIMON. After the hitting I was, yes.

(A beat.)

CAREY. Um, honey?

SIMON. Yes, lambchop?

CAREY. You look stupid.

SIMON. Thank you. Now go and be pregnant somewhere else.

CAREY. What's with the disguise?

SIMON. My eyes were bugging me, so I pumped myself full of drugs and blocked out all the light. Never felt better.

CAREY. Maybe we should make you another appointment with Dr. Rose.

SIMON. I'm telling you, it's a penis.

(SIMON *holds up the ultrasound photo.*)

CAREY. It's not a penis.

SIMON. I think it might be.

CAREY. Well then our child has a penis growing out of her arm.

SIMON. His arm.

CAREY. I'm positive it's a girl.

SIMON. I think so too.

CAREY. What?

SIMON. I agree with you.

CAREY. Why have you spent the last four days defending an opinion you don't actually hold?

SIMON. Because I find conflict sssexy.

CAREY. Well I find being right sssexy.

SIMON. Well then, we're both feelin' sssexy right now.

CAREY. Not really. Too bloated. I'll give you this though.

(*She lifts up her shirt and flashes him.*)

For the spank bank.

(SIMON *picks up the jar and holds it out.*)

What?

SIMON. That is filthy. That's worse than swearing.

CAREY. Spank's safe, bank's safe and context doesn't matter.

SIMON. So many rules.

> (**SIMON** *pulls her into a hug and kisses her neck.*)

I love your rules.

> (*He holds her here in stillness, with his face buried in her neck.*)

CAREY. Did you take ecstasy?

SIMON. So, if the penis-armed baby is in fact a girl, what should we name her? 'Cause I still like Gretchen.

CAREY. "Gretchen." "Gretch." "Hey Gretch, go fetch." Nope, too many dog jokes.

SIMON. Uh... "That Gretchen, she's fetchin'."

CAREY. "Hey Gretchen! Where's Hansel?"

SIMON. What?

CAREY. I much prefer Rachel.

SIMON. Rachel. (*In a mean-girl voice.*) "Rachel!"

CAREY. Yeah.

SIMON. "Come here, Rachel – you're a...you smell like a..." Yeah, Rachel's okay, I guess.

CAREY. Thank you for forgiving me.

SIMON. For what?

CAREY. For turning into a raging psychopath.

SIMON. Ohhh, that. Anytime. I need another coffee – you want one?

CAREY. I'm pregnant.

SIMON. Again?! Does this mean it's twins?!

CAREY. No caffeine.

SIMON. Right. Wine?

CAREY. Pregnant.

SIMON. Meth?

CAREY. Pregnant.

SIMON. Unpasteurized dairy products?

CAREY. Go away forever.

(*He exits into to the kitchen. She studies the ultrasound again.*)

What if it is a boy?

SIMON. (*Offstage.*) We sell it.

CAREY. I'm talking about names.

SIMON. (*Offstage.*) "Gretchen" is nice.

(**CAREY** *groans.*)

How about "Seitan"?

CAREY. Satan?

SIMON. (*Offstage.*) Seitan. Like the vegetarian meat substitute.

CAREY. What is *wrong* with you?

SIMON. (*Offstage.*) You're the one who eats that shit.

CAREY. That's five dollars. Was it worth it?

SIMON. (*Offstage.*) You're the one who eats that...poo.

CAREY. You are so unsupportive of my vegetarianism.

SIMON. (*Offstage.*) You can't eat chicken and then say you're a vegetarian.

CAREY. I'm a chickotarian.

(Silence.)

Tough crowd.

(More silence.)

Simon?

*(In the world of the bookstore, **OWEN** takes a seat on the floor, practicing his ad-libbed mournful guitar song from Scene Twelve.)*

Maybe I *should* have coffee. Maybe caffeine would make me funnier.

(Silence.)

Are you ignoring me? Simon?

*(**CAREY** gets up and peeks into the kitchen, as **OWEN** continues playing.)*

*(**CAREY** sees **SIMON** offstage. Her face falls.)*

Oh my god, Simon...

(She runs into the kitchen, exiting the stage.)

*(**OWEN** continues playing until he has finished the song, then sets down his guitar.)*

Scene Fourteen

(A memory.)

(The bookstore.)

*(**OWEN** is sorting through a pile of books. **CAREY** approaches him and waits for him to acknowledge her. He doesn't.)*

CAREY. I'm sorry for coming to your work. I didn't really know how else to... I left a few messages. I'm not sure if you got them.

OWEN. This isn't a great time...

CAREY. I just wanted to clear up a few things.

OWEN. It's not a good time.

> *(**CAREY** nods and starts to walk away. **OWEN** stops her.)*

Why did you lie?

CAREY. I – I didn't lie, it's not...

> *(She searches.)*

I withheld information.

OWEN. Why would you kiss me, if you were – I mean, why does someone do something like that, if they're married?

CAREY. It's not that simple.

OWEN. It never is with you.

CAREY. *(Annoyed.)* You're right. We should do this another time.

OWEN. I just, I liked you a lot. You know?

CAREY. I'm sorry.

OWEN. I don't want sympathy. That's not –

CAREY. I don't want sympathy either.

OWEN. For *what*?

CAREY. I'm gonna say this, and then I'm gonna go.

> (**OWEN** *waits.*)

I'm not married. I was married, I feel married. But I'm not. He died, my husband.

> (**OWEN** *stands completely still, overcome with sadness. The silence between them lasts for a full ten seconds.*)

Huh.

OWEN. *(Softly.)* What?

CAREY. You just – you didn't say "sorry."

OWEN. Sorry?

CAREY. Everyone always apologizes when I tell them, which makes the repressed standup comic in me want to say, "Why, did you kill him?"

> (*Still nothing from* **OWEN**.)

I always thought it would be nice for someone to just stay quiet.

OWEN. *(Quietly.)* How long has it been?

CAREY. No time. A lifetime. Three years. Well, it was three years on May the fourth.

OWEN. May the –

CAREY. *(Stiffening.)* I'm gonna head out now and maybe we can talk later. About art or clowns or something. Anything other than this, 'kay? I'd rather not talk about this.

(She starts to leave, then turns to face **OWEN** *again.)*

I'm sorry for kissing you. I liked you too.

(She exits to the world of the concert.)

Scene Fifteen

(The concert.)

*(Alone, **CAREY** takes a sip of her drink and sets it down. She looks around for **OWEN**. There is no sign of him.)*

CAREY. Simon and I once agreed that his thirtieth birthday was the worst day of our entire relationship. I forgot that it was his birthday, and in an unforgivable reversal of roles, *he* brought *me* breakfast in bed – huevos rancheros *muy caliente*, just the way I like it – which I proceeded to spill onto our white Calvin Klein duvet. I yelled at him for handing me my plate before I was ready and he locked himself in his study and wrote a short story about a Mexican witch.

When I realized that I had completely forgotten his thirtieth birthday, I whipped up a surprise chocolate cake. Unfortunately, I accidentally mixed my earring into the batter, and Simon spent the remainder of his birthday having emergency dental surgery. Simon brought this up many times, over many years, but I don't think I ever really apologized.

*(**OWEN** joins **CAREY** on stage holding a fresh drink. She nods at him.)*

Neither of us was very good at apologies.

*(**OWEN** heads for his guitar and takes a seat, watching the next scene unfold from his post.)*

Scene Sixteen

(A memory.)

(Simon and Carey's living room.)

(CAREY sorts through a large pile of suits. She examines them one by one as BEV joins her holding two mugs of coffee.)

BEV. I know the hippies say you're not supposed to have caffeine when you're pregnant, but once in a while...

(She hands CAREY a mug.)

I figured a little Kahlúa wouldn't hurt either.

CAREY. Thanks.

(CAREY finds a chocolate bar wrapper in of one of Simon's pockets.)

Oh Simon, gross. *(Holding it up.)* In his pocket.

(CAREY gets up to throw the wrapper away. She stands at the garbage can for a moment staring at the wrapper, but can't bring herself to part with it. She folds it up and puts it in her pocket.)

BEV. Why don't you take a break from all that now?

CAREY. I don't know how to do this.

BEV. I know, dear.

CAREY. I don't know what to do.

(BEV wells up, struggling to maintain composure.)

God, I'm sorry – are you okay? Do you want something? A sandwich?

BEV. No thanks. I've been doing... *(Shaking her head.)* Seems ludicrous now.

CAREY. I could use a little bit of ludicrous.

BEV. It's a new diet. No sandwiches.

CAREY. That's very specific.

> *(**BEV** manages a smile.)*

CAREY. I said to Simon that you looked different, but we couldn't tell what it...

> *(Losing herself in the memory of him.)*

...uh...what it was. He thought maybe it was because of the quitting. The smoking.

BEV. Oh, what a good idea.

> *(**BEV** stands up and goes to her coat. She takes a pack of cigarettes out of her pocket then walks over to **CAREY**.)*

I know I'm not always the warmest. Not always the best. But I'm here for you, for your daughter. Or son.

> *(She holds up the cigarette.)*

I'm going to smoke this now. I'm going to take it outside, and light it, and smoke it.

> *(**BEV** smiles at **CAREY** then heads outside.)*

> *(**CAREY** picks up one of Simon's suit jackets and studies it, then lays it down on the floor. She picks up another blazer, gives it a once-over and adds it to the pile.)*

> *(She holds up the tweed jacket that Simon was wearing at the beginning of the play. She lays it down flat in front of her and runs her hands over the pockets, noticing something*

inside. She takes out the yellow piece of paper and unfolds it. She reads it, stunned.)

CAREY. Bev? BEV.

*(**BEV** rushes back in.)*

BEV. Are you alright?

CAREY. This...this is –

*(**CAREY**, speechless, holds out the piece of paper. **BEV** takes it and scans the contents.)*

BEV. *(Softly.)* Oh my dear.

CAREY. This is just sitting in his pocket? In with the candy wrappers and the fucking – sorry. Did you read it?

BEV. Just the beginning.

CAREY. Those are not good results. Berry aneurysm? I don't even –

*(**CAREY** takes the piece of paper back from **BEV**.)*

Is that what it – ?

BEV. Carey.

CAREY. He must not have read this, right? The doctor must have forgotten to – Simon must never have seen this. I have to call Dr. Rose.

BEV. It's not her fault.

CAREY. Then whose fault is it? He wouldn't have kept this from us, Bev. There was a family history. She should be sued.

BEV. Maybe he *did* know.

CAREY. You don't understand. He told me everything. I got detailed updates on his bowel movements for fuck's sake – for god's sake. For FUCK'S SAKE.

BEV. You're pregnant.

CAREY. I'm fine.

BEV. No, I mean, maybe he felt that in your condition, you couldn't handle the news.

CAREY. The news that he was DYING? Simon doesn't lie, Bev. He didn't lie. He told me everything.

BEV. Well he didn't tell you this.

(*Silence.*)

CAREY. I'm sorry, I'm gonna need you to spell this out for me. You're saying that he knew he was sick?

BEV. (*Quietly.*) Yes.

CAREY. But he didn't know, obviously, how sick.

(*Silence.*)

He couldn't have known how sick. Right?

BEV. He should have told you.

CAREY. I asked him to his face. He looked me in the face and he swore.

BEV. I don't know if it was denial, or –

CAREY. He told *you*? Why would he tell you?

BEV. Because I am his mother.

CAREY. Then why didn't you tell me?

BEV. He asked me not to. And I am his mother. He is my son.

(**BEV** *stiffens, refusing to become emotional.*)

We have to help each other through this.

CAREY. I will never get through this. My husband is dead. And now you're telling me that I didn't know him. That he kept secrets from me and made decisions behind my back. That he lied to me.

BEV. We wanted to protect you.

CAREY. Well you didn't do a very good job, did you?

(*A beat.*)

I need you to leave.

BEV. I'll come by tomorrow.

CAREY. No you won't.

BEV. Carey, please. I have no one else to –

(*A beat.*)

I'll come by tomorrow.

(**BEV** *exits.*)

Scene Seventeen

(The concert.)

[MUSIC NO. 06 "FAMILY"]

*(***OWEN*** *plays an upbeat, chugging introduction.* ***CAREY*** *sings.)*

CAREY.
    MY SISTER DOESN'T CALL ENOUGH
    MY FATHER WAS A LUSH
    MY GRANDPA NEVER SENT US CASH
    YOUR MOTHER SENT TOO MUCH
    AND WE'D COMPLAIN AT CHRISTMASTIME
    TOO MANY GIFTS TO BUY
    BUT SECRETLY WE KNEW WE WERE
    SO LUCKY, YOU AND I.

    (Simon and Carey's living room begins to transform. By the end of the song, the furniture has been rearranged and the floor is littered with toddler toys.)

OUR DAUGHTER CAME INTO THIS WORLD
NINE POUNDS OF WAILING JOY
SHE HAD MY HAIR, YOUR EYES, MY NOSE
AND FAR TOO MANY TOYS
BUT BARBIES COME AND BARBIES GO
AND TRAINS LOSE THEIR ALLURE
THE ONLY THING SHE WON'T OUTGROW
IS HER PHOTOGRAPH OF YOU

Scene Eighteen

(A memory.)

(Carey's living room, littered with toys.)

*(**OWEN** hovers in the doorway.)*

OWEN. I hope this isn't too bold.

CAREY. Bold is good. I like bold.

OWEN. Thank you for your message. I appreciated that.

CAREY. Good, good. I was worried that maybe I offended you with the whole "let's be friends" thing.

OWEN. That wasn't my favorite part.

(He notices something on the floor behind her.)

Do you have a train fetish?

CAREY. No, they're – they actually belong to my...

OWEN. Son?

CAREY. Daughter.

OWEN. Cool.

(A beat.)

I don't think you mentioned that.

CAREY. I didn't want to lay all of it on you at once.

OWEN. You didn't lay any of it on me ever.

CAREY. I'm working on being more open. Please, come in.

OWEN. Is your daughter home?

CAREY. It's fine – she's napping. It always takes her a few hours to recover from her hockey lesson, so...

OWEN. She plays hockey?

CAREY. Well, it's the three-and-under category, so it's less like hockey and more like toddler dominoes on ice. But...yep.

(**CAREY** *sits on the couch.* **OWEN** *follows suit.*)

OWEN. So that was your mother-in-law that we ran into?

CAREY. Bev. Yeah.

OWEN. Is she okay?

CAREY. I don't really know. That was the first time I've seen her in a while.

OWEN. She lives out of town, or – ?

(**CAREY** *fidgets.*)

Sorry, I didn't mean to overstep.

CAREY. It's fine. I have no problem talking about it, about anything.

OWEN. Well except that you –

CAREY. I haven't seen her since before the funeral.

OWEN. She didn't go to the funeral?

CAREY. I didn't go.

OWEN. So how did you say goodbye?

CAREY. To her?

OWEN. To him.

(*Uncomfortable,* **CAREY** *starts cleaning up the living room.*)

I like you.

CAREY. I can't –

OWEN. *Listen.*

CAREY. Okay.

OWEN. I like you. And I want to be your friend. You kept some important stuff from me and I still don't totally understand that, but I'm not going anywhere. So...if you need advice or someone to talk to, I'm your man. Person.

CAREY. Thank you.

OWEN. My first piece of advice, for instance, would be that you should get in touch with your mother-in-law.

CAREY. *(Sarcastic.)* Don't hold back.

OWEN. Feeling guilty all the time, it's no way to live.

CAREY. She's a bad influence. She – I don't know, she – she's unemotional and she smokes, and –

OWEN. I smoke marijuana now and then.

CAREY. That's fine. I would too, but it makes my eyelids puff up.

OWEN. You should phone her.

CAREY. She lied to me.

OWEN. People lie.

>   *(Silence.)*

CAREY. I tried. Once. Well, I phoned. I didn't talk to her, but I left her a message.

OWEN. That's good.

CAREY. I didn't say any actual words, but...

>   *(**OWEN** gives her a look.)*

I know! I panicked when I heard the beep, so I just kind of cleared my throat and hung up.

OWEN. Gotta start somewhere.

(They smile at each other.)

Oh! I was wondering – would you like to play with me sometime? *(Off* **CAREY***'s reaction.)* Music, play music.

CAREY. I would love that. I actually haven't done much singing since – yeah. So...

(She holds out her hand for a handshake.)

...friends?

*(***OWEN*** takes her hand.)*

OWEN. Friends.

(They shake hands.)

*(***OWEN*** turns to go, but* **CAREY** *won't let go of his hand. She pulls him in and kisses him, hard. They hold each other close, kissing passionately as the lights shift.)*

Scene Nineteen

(A memory.)

(Carey's living room.)

(**BEV** *is holding a fancy-looking envelope.*)

BEV. I don't understand this.

CAREY. It's a birthday invitation.

BEV. You're throwing him a birthday party?

CAREY. A birthday-party-slash-concert-slash-wake.

BEV. Bit late for all that, isn't it?

CAREY. It is, yes.

BEV. Why did you send one to me?

CAREY. Because Simon would have wanted you to be there.

BEV. I see. And when did that become important?

CAREY. Bev...

BEV. Simon would have wanted me to know my granddaughter, too.

CAREY. I made a mistake.

BEV. A mistake? No. Buying a twin sheet for a double bed is a mistake. Skipping your husband's funeral, abandoning his only living relative, not allowing his mother to meet her grandchild when she has no one else in the world – that is not a mistake. That is an abomination.

CAREY. *Allowing* you to meet her? You knew where to find me. You never –

BEV. Don't put this on me.

CAREY. I was in shock, Bev. I didn't just lose Simon. I lost all of our memories. Everything was tainted.

BEV. My son made a decision and I had to respect it.

CAREY. I understand that now that I'm a mother. I understand a lot of things now that I'm a m –

BEV. But he was wrong. We were wrong.

> *(A beat.)*

I have racked my brain trying to figure it out, and all I can think is that he didn't want anything to change. He wanted his life with you to stay the same. No sympathy, no fear. Does that make any sense?

CAREY. I don't know.

BEV. What you two had was...a rare and miraculous thing.

> *(**CAREY** cannot bring herself to look at **BEV**.)*

CAREY. I know that what I did to you was unforgivable. I just needed someone to – I don't know.

BEV. To blame.

CAREY. Yes.

BEV. So did I. I would like to meet my granddaughter.

CAREY. You will. You can. She knows all about you.

BEV. Oh dear...

CAREY. Well, she knows that you are Daddy's mother. And that you make a world-famous pecan pie.

BEV. *(Concerned.)* I buy those. But I could certainly heat one up.

> *(She looks around.)*

The house looks very smart. The couch looks nice over there.

CAREY. Thanks, I –

> (**CAREY**'s *phone rings. She checks it, then gets uncomfortable and declines the call.*)

> (**BEV** *holds up the invitation.*)

BEV. This is... I may not be able to make it to this.

CAREY. Okay. Whatever you need.

BEV. I have tennis. I'm taking lessons.

CAREY. At night?

BEV. All the time.

> (**CAREY**'s *cell phone rings again.*)

CAREY. He's persistent.

> (*She awkwardly silences the call.*)

BEV. Is that your boyfriend?

CAREY. Oh, I don't have a –

BEV. I swore off men after The Cancer.

CAREY. My god, I didn't know you'd had –

BEV. Lord no, not the disease. That's what I call my ex-husband. Needless to say, I may not be the person to turn to for romantic advice.

CAREY. Oh, I'm not looking for – it's casual with Owen. That was too much information. I'm in love with Simon, is what I'm saying. You can't be in love with two people at once.

BEV. Unless they are both very rich.

> (*She tries not to smile.*)

Will he be at this "concert"?

CAREY. Who? Oh. Well if not it'll be a very short concert.

(**BEV** *looks confused.*)

He's accompanying me. My guitar skills are...lacking.

BEV. I remember.

(*Silence.*)

If you had been the one to die, what would Simon have done?

CAREY. If I had –? He would have been a great parent, for starters. Better than I am.

(*A beat.*)

He would have moved on, I know that. But it's a different – everything would have been different. I would have told him the truth about the aneurysm, we would have gone through it together. We would have had a plan.

BEV. Simon only confided in me twice in his life. Did you know that? Once about his diagnosis, and once about Mr. Greenwood.

CAREY. Mr. *Greenwood*?

BEV. Simon thought you had feelings for him.

CAREY. (*Laughing.*) Mr. Greenwood wore bow ties!

BEV. He was a co-worker, he had a nice singing voice, he had some kind of accent. Simon said you liked accents.

CAREY. It's true, I do.

BEV. Well, he was concerned.

CAREY. I used to *joke* about having a crush on Mr. Greenwood. I'm glad he was jealous, though. He never got jealous.

BEV. Oh, he wasn't jealous. He was *concerned* because he felt you could do better.

(**CAREY** *laughs.* **BEV** *takes* **CAREY**'s *hands.*)

All he thought about, all he cared about was you. So go after what you want.

CAREY. What do I want?

Scene Twenty

(The concert venue – a rehearsal.)

(OWEN shows CAREY around the space.)

OWEN. So, the audience will be out here. Obviously.

CAREY. It's bigger than I expected.

OWEN. You'll be great.

CAREY. My biggest audience ever was twenty. And their median age was ten.

OWEN. At least here they allow drinking and cursing.

CAREY. "Cursing," huh? I thought no one under the age of eighty used that word...

OWEN. *(Confused.)* I never said that.

> *(OWEN continues the tour. CAREY is distracted.)*

We'll either be sitting here or over there.

CAREY. Thanks for doing this. I know it's a bit weird.

OWEN. Naaaah.

CAREY. *(Amused.)* It's not weird?

OWEN. Naaaaah. Totally normal.

CAREY. The guy I'm sleeping with playing guitar at my husband's wake?

OWEN. The guy you're – yikes.

CAREY. You know what I mean.

> *(OWEN tries to shake it off. He gestures toward the living room set.)*

OWEN. Uh, so hopefully, this'll all be gone.

CAREY. Owen...

OWEN. It's okay, it's fine. Why don't we practice the new song.

CAREY. Yeah, let me just go through the lyrics once...

> (**CAREY** *stands on the stage looking out at the "empty" theatre. She sings, in rehearsal mode.*)

[MUSIC NO. 07 "FORGETTING YOUR FACE"]

WHAT KIND OF SPECIES ARE WE
THAT WE HATE TO GROW
WE –

OWEN. "The guy you're sleeping with"? Seriously?

CAREY. No...

> (**CAREY** *walks over to* **OWEN** *and puts her arms around him.*)

I didn't mean it like that. I'm an a-hole.

> (*She kisses him. He smiles.*)

OWEN. Maybe a tiny one.

CAREY. A tiny a-hole? Is that better or worse?

OWEN.	**CAREY.**
I don't really wanna –	Let's never think about –

> (*They laugh.*)

OWEN. Keep singin', a-hole. I need to practice this chord progression.

> (**CAREY** *sits down on the stage, her legs dangling over the edge.*)

CAREY.

    WHAT KIND OF SPECIES ARE WE
    THAT WE HATE TO GROW
    WE SEE OUR DEATHS UP AHEAD
    BUT DON'T WANT TO KNOW

OWEN. How does the chorus go again?

CAREY. There is no chorus.

OWEN. That's a bold choice.

CAREY. You can write one, if you want.

OWEN. Really?

CAREY. Of course, yeah. We're in this together.

    *(She smiles at him – honestly, openly. He melts. **CAREY** continues singing out to the house.)*

    THE STEAM RISES FROM MY WET SKIN
    MY TOWEL'S OUT OF REACH
    WHY DO I ALWAYS FORGET
    THE THING I MOST NEED

OWEN. *(Matter-of factly.)* I love you.

    *(**CAREY** wheels around, stunned.)*

Scene Twenty-One

(A lighting shift. The song continues, now in the world of the concert.)

*(**OWEN** and **CAREY** have more distance between them. **OWEN** rocks out on the guitar as he and **CAREY** sing the chorus.)*

OWEN & CAREY.

FEAR GETS ME DOWN
AND FEAR GETS ME BY
AND FEAR STOPS MY HEART
AND FEAR LEARNS TO FLY
FEAR'S WINNING THE RACE
I'M CHEERING FEAR ON
FORGETTING YOUR FACE
IS TORMENT

CAREY.

WHAT KIND OF SPECIES ARE WE
THAT WE HATE TO GROW
WE SEE A DOOR UP AHEAD
BUT WE WANT IT CLOSED
AND WHEN THE BATTLE'S BEEN WON
WE LONG TO BE FREE
BUT WE DIDN'T SHOW UP TO FIGHT
WE WATCHED ON TV

OWEN & CAREY.

AND FEAR GETS US DOWN
AND FEAR GETS US THROUGH
AND FEAR SAVES OUR HEARTS
AND FEAR KEEPS US TRUE
FEAR'S WINNING THE RACE
AND I DON'T OBJECT
'CAUSE WINNING THE RACE

MEANS LOSING
'CAUSE WINNING THE RACE
MEANS LOSING
'CAUSE WINNING THE RACE
MEANS LOSING

CAREY.
...YOU

Scene Twenty-Two

(The concert venue – a rehearsal.)

*(**CAREY** and **OWEN** are mid-argument.)*

CAREY. If you want to back out, I understand. I can accompany myself.

OWEN. No you can't.

CAREY. Owen, it's way too soon to be telling each other we –

OWEN. So this isn't going anywhere? We're just...screwing?

CAREY. "Screwing." That's awful. You make it sound like –

OWEN. – we're having an affair? That's exactly how it feels.

CAREY. We are having an affair! I'm cheating on him. Do you understand that?

OWEN. He's dead, Carey. He's gone.

CAREY. God, Owen, if you say stuff like that, there's no going back. We can't ever –

OWEN. Say stuff like what? It's the truth. And it's been *three years*. It's okay for you to –

CAREY. If you say "move on" I will punch you in the crotch.

OWEN. I was going to say "be happy."

(A beat.)

Listen, I'm an idiot for telling you I love you – I take it back. It's too soon. I understand that. But you're not doing anything wrong here.

CAREY. I know that! But I regret it. All of it. I regret sleeping with you...

OWEN. That's nice. Thank you for that.

CAREY. No, it was great! It was amazing. You do things to me that I have never...that's not the point.

(*A beat.*)

Everything was going so well. My job's fine, I don't cry every day, I'm a reasonably good mother. It took me so long to find my way. And when I'm with you, I feel like I'm lost again. I'm just – I'm lost.

OWEN. What's wrong with being lost?

Scene Twenty-Three

(The concert.)

*(**CAREY** steps forward, holding the swearing jar.)*

CAREY. As many of you know, today would have been Simon's fortieth birthday. I would probably have teased him for being old, but he was also, undeniably, much too young.

Before we finish off, I would like to make a bit of an announcement. It's been just over three years since Simon and I started this and I'm half proud and half horrified to say that even after throwing this party, it still holds $2,700.00. So I've decided that the rest of the money will go towards a vacation for myself and my daughter, Gretchen. She's not even three yet, but she is a fan of Jay the Jet Plane, so I think she'll be pleased.

I would also like to take this opportunity to thank my dear friend, Owen, for playing and singing so beautifully.

And last but not least, I would like to thank my husband, Simon, for bringing joy to my life every day for twelve years. And to the lives of every person he met for thirty-seven years. Happy birthday, Simon.

*(In the world of the concert, **CAREY** turns and sees **SIMON** asleep on the couch. She crosses into the living room, joins him on the couch and runs her fingers through his hair. He wakes up.)*

SIMON. Hey.

CAREY. Hi...

SIMON. When did you get home?

CAREY. Couple of hours ago. Since when do you take afternoon naps, old timer?

SIMON. I had a wicked headache.

CAREY. *(Doing her best surfer impression.)* WICKED.

SIMON. No.

CAREY. Are you okay now?

SIMON. Yep. Are yous okay?

CAREY. "Yous"?

> *(He gesturse to her stomach.)*

Oh. Yes. We's is fine. Me and Rachel.

SIMON. Gretchen.

CAREY. Rachel.

SIMON. I'm too weak to fight.

CAREY. Score!

> *(She lies down with her head in his lap.)*

SIMON. If anything ever happens to me...

CAREY. I am not having this conversation.

SIMON. ...I want you to take a vow of celibacy.

CAREY. You are the love of my life, you asshole.

SIMON. That's five dollars in the –

CAREY. It's in the kitchen. And it's full.

SIMON. You know that I wouldn't want you to be alone, right?

> *(She sits up and looks him in the eye.)*

CAREY. I will never, ever love anyone else.

(In the world of the concert, **OWEN** *begins to play.)*

[MUSIC NO. 08 "THE TURTLE"]

*(***SIMON*** *stands up and slowly moves away from* **CAREY***. She holds his hand for as long as she can until it slips through her fingers. He walks away and does not look back. When* **SIMON** *is gone,* **CAREY** *sings.)*

AND I
AN OLD TURTLE
WILL WING ME TO SOME WITHER'D BOUGH
AND THERE MY MATE
THAT'S NEVER TO BE FOUND AGAIN
LAMENT 'TIL I AM...

*(***CAREY*** *turns and looks at* **OWEN***, as though seeing him clearly for the first time.)*

...LOST.

The End

Printed in the USA
CPSIA information can be obtained
at www.ICGtesting.com
LVHW020204251023
762075LV00007B/193